George Patton F

The Life and Military Career

of the Legendary General

"A Pint of Sweat Will Save a Gallon of Blood."

-   George Patton -

By Ryan T Cox

Copyright © 2023 by Ryan T Cox
All rights reserved.

The content of this book may not be reproduced, duplicated, or transmitted without the author's or publisher's express written permission. Under no circumstances will the publisher or author be held liable or legally responsible for any damages, reparation, or monetary loss caused by the information contained in this book, whether directly or indirectly.

Legal Notice:

This publication is copyrighted. It is strictly for personal use only. You may not change, distribute, sell, use, quote, or paraphrase any part of this book without the author's or publisher's permission.

Disclaimer Notice:

Please keep in mind that the information in this document is only for educational and entertainment purposes. Every effort has been made to present accurate, up-to-date, reliable, and comprehensive information. There are no express or implied warranties. Readers understand that the author is not providing legal, financial, medical, or professional advice. This book's content was compiled from a variety of sources. Please seek the advice of a licensed professional before attempting any of the techniques described in this book. By reading this document, the reader agrees that the author is not liable for any direct or indirect losses incurred as a result of using the information contained within this document, including, but not limited to, errors, omissions, or inaccuracies.

TABLE OF CONTENTS

INTRODUCTION

CHAPTER 1: A Patent for Patton

CHAPTER 2: In Between War

CHAPTER 3: This Means War

CHAPTER 4: Operation Husky

CHAPTER 5: Invasion of Normandy

CHAPTER 6: The Battle of the Bulge

CHAPTER 7: An Old Man's War

CHAPTER 8: Watch Your Mouth

CHAPTER 9: Man of Controversy

CHAPTER 10: The Last Days of Patton

CONCLUSION

INTRODUCTION

General George S. Patton, a symbol of pride and controversy, is generally viewed as someone who was both crass and eloquent; heroic and diabolical. How could someone so famous generate such a dichotomy in public perception?

In reality, General Patton's bizarre dichotomy appeared to begin when he was a tiny child. His dualism of spirit seemed to develop as he listened to his father's and war veteran friends' nightly stories. Hearing their accounts of infantry charges and heroic gallantry in battle, the young Patton began to fantasize about filling their enormous shoes.

The power of his imagination was so strong that he could see himself battling with his forefathers. This visual exercise would lead him to accept the concept of reincarnation, launching a lifetime belief that he had previously lived, fighting in battles in the distant past.

Later in life, he was famous for entertaining his companions with stories of hypothetical past lives he might have had fighting for Rome's Legions or as a trooper in Napoleon's artillery. Regardless of his spiritual leanings, whether he lived one life or a billion, his spirit was unquestionably bigger than them all.

CHAPTER 1:
A Patent for Patton

"May God have mercy on my enemies, because I won't."

- *General George S. Patton* -

The birthday of the legendary American General George S. Patton was not a special occasion. On November 11, 1885, he arrived in San Gabriel, California, at the home of his already well-established military family. Twenty years had elapsed since the end of the American Civil War, in which many of Patton's Virginia ancestors had fought on the losing side.

With the most lethal and catastrophic of American conflicts behind it, the country appeared to be reveling in its newfound tranquility. Instead of fighting deadly wars and ripping the country apart, most Americans were more concerned at the time with preserving and conserving what they already had.

The Washington Monument was dedicated for the first time in 1885, and Niagara Falls State Park was formed the same year. In contrast to the serious turmoil that the nation faced in 1865, the year of Patton's birth, most Americans could sense a general satisfaction and gratitude for the resources that this nation—just over a century old at the time—had to offer.

Even though he was born into a peaceful society, it didn't take long for a young "Georgie," as his parents called him, to develop an interest in weapons of war. Patton's favorite hobby as a child growing up on ranches in Southern California was riding horses across the range, imagining himself leading daring cavalry attacks against his adversaries.

Patton would leave the ranches of California at the age of 18 to attend the Virginia Military Academy, which his predecessors had attended. His time at VMI would be brief, and with the help of a letter of reference from California Senator T.G. Bard, he would be on his way to the most prestigious military training facility of all: West Point.

Patton appeared to be at ease and eager to thrive on this sacred field of military training at first. But, Patton would soon face a formidable foe: mathematics. The future General, who would surge over Europe against unbelievable odds, was struggling to solve basic numerical calculations. His grades were so poor that he had to retake his freshman year.
He was able to eventually defeat his mathematical adversary the following year via determined and intensive study over his summer holiday. Patton graduated from West Point on June 11th, 1909, rated 46th out of 103 students. With his academic record intact, the world seemed ready for George Patton to seize.

After successfully completing his studies at West Point, Patton was awarded the post of second lieutenant in the United States Cavalry, a field that would later lead him to his actual destiny as a tank commander when horses were phased out by mechanized combat.

Patton would find himself momentarily settling down, marrying, and having children at this point in his life. On May 26th, 1910, he married his lifelong love, Beatrice Ayer, with whom he had two daughters and one son. His military career would then take him to Fort Sheridan, close outside Chicago, in September 1910. Patton's life would take another unexpected turn here, only three years into his service, when his superiors chose him for—of all things—the 1912 Olympics.

The current Olympic Games had just recently been resurrected less than a decade previously, in 1896. Patton was chosen to represent the United States in the fourth Olympics because of his great fencing and running abilities, which he had already shown during his time at West Point.

Three years after his Olympic exploits, George Patton was relocated from Fort Sheridan to Fort Bliss, Texas, just across the border from Mexico. He became involved in border conflicts between US forces and Mexican criminals who routinely raided border villages.

The border situation deteriorated over time, culminating in March 1916 when Mexican General Pancho Villa dispatched around 100 fighters across the border to lay siege to Columbus, New Mexico. Villa devastated the 13th Cavalry Regiment of the United States in this surprise attack, seizing roughly 100 horses and a large range of military equipment before torching the entire town.

To say that both the US military and the general public were taken aback would be an understatement. This was the first major foreign force assault on American land since the British attacked in 1812, and it was an instance of outside aggression that would not be replicated until the Japanese bombed Hawaii on December 7th, 1941. Having said that, the United States government took this raid very seriously. As a response, then-President Woodrow Wilson directed the crossing of the border and capture of Pancho Villa by 5000 US forces. General John Pershing was tasked with leading the charge, and it was Pershing who soon after enlisted George Patton to help him, eventually making him a vital element of the 13th Cavalry, the very unit that had been looted by Pancho Villa.

Patton's first expedition into combat occurred here on May 14, 1916, when he drove ten soldiers and two civilian scouts across the Mexican border in three Dodge touring vehicles. Patton and his soldiers didn't waste any time in locating and overtaking a group of Villa's militants, killing three of them in the process. Patton achieved a quick reputation in the press, which began to refer to him as the "bandit slayer."

Despite this early victory over Villa's bandits, Pancho Villa remained at loose, and the mission was called off in February 1917. Patton didn't have to wait long because the winds of change were blowing in Europe, and a series of events would soon launch half of the world into World War One.

Patton's old mentor Pershing was commissioned as the commander of the American Expeditionary Force (AEF) in the fight here. Following in the footsteps of Pershing, Patton was dispatched to the Western Front on May 15, 1917, to join him. Patton would meet the newly-minted motorized military behemoth known as the tank for the first time here.

During his time in Europe, he attended a French tank school, which vastly increased his understanding and enthusiasm for the subject. Patton's interest in tanks would soon pay dividends when he was appointed first officer in the newly formed United States Tank Corps. Patton quickly rose through the ranks of tank repair and planning.

Once World War One ended, Patton's beloved Tank Corps was temporarily disbanded, but not before Patton requested to his superiors that if the corps ever returned, he would be placed at its helm. This was a request that would inevitably propel Patton into the history books decades later, when the world would be embroiled in another world war, even more terrible than the first.

CHAPTER 2:
In Between War

"A pint of sweat will save a gallon of blood."

- General George S. Patton-

Life between the battlements of war was a battle in and of itself for George S. Patton. Patton, never one to sit idle during peacetime, jumped headfirst into a wide range of postings, responsibilities, and businesses. Most notably, in 1920, he worked in Washington, D.C. on a project to create one of the first user guides in the form of instruction manuals on operating military tanks.

It was around this time that Patton met future General and President Dwight D. Eisenhower for the first time. They quickly formed a friendship that would endure the remainder of Patton's life. Apart from Eisenhower, Patton encountered numerous people during the interwar period who would play an important role in molding his later career. Despite his success in climbing the social ladder of his professional environment, Patton quickly felt dissatisfied with the life of a peacetime staff officer.

When he was redeployed to Hawaii in 1925, he would soon relish a getaway from all of the D.C. political hobnobbing and intrigue that surrounded him. According to all accounts, the Pattons fell in love with living on the Hawaiian Islands, and it was a wonderful opportunity for them to reconnect as a family. Years later, General George Patton's son would recall fondly how he and his father would comb the beaches flying model airplanes and taking lengthy excursions in the ocean.

But good things must come to an end, and the Patton family was issued the marching orders to return to Washington just a few years later, in 1928. Returning to D.C. Patton was given the title "Chief of

Cavalry," a position that required Patton to travel from one site to another overseeing the forces over which he had command.

Patton hoped to carry up where he left off when it came to integrating mechanized combat with more traditional cavalry brigades in this capacity of overseer. He aimed to combine artillery, infantry, and cavalry into a single fully mechanized formation. Patton was first given free rein to test his concept, but due to a sudden drop in funds from the United States Congress, he was forced to abandon his plans.

Patton's life became pretty regular after his objectives were briefly thwarted. The sole break from his postwar depression in the following years came in the form of a large protest of veterans marching on the capital in the summer of 1932. The unhappy veterans, dubbed the "Bonus Expeditionary Force" in mock parody of the American Expeditionary Force in which they served during World War One, were out of work and seeking recompense.

Many of them were given certificates in 1924 that guaranteed them future bonus payments that could be redeemed by 1945. Most of these veterans were fed up with the Great Depression of the 1930s and, rather than waiting another decade for their promised commission, took to the streets to demand immediate cash payment for the money they had been promised.

Most of these guys served alongside Patton on the Western Front, and he very doubt sympathized with their cause, but as a steadfast soldier, he couldn't ignore his instructions. On July 28th, he set aside his feelings for his old comrades in arms and led a charge against the protesters, pushing them away from the White House with bayonets and tear gas.

Patton subsequently admitted that he was appalled by the treatment of the veterans, but that it was a necessary evil at the moment to prevent what he believed would become an "armed insurgency" against the United States government. Patton's uncompromising adherence to these harsh rules would soon pay off in 1934, when he was promoted to Lieutenant Colonel and sent back to his home Hawaii.

It was here that he rekindle his interest in the foreign politics that were changing the world. From Hawaii, in particular, he began to keep a careful eye on happenings across the Pacific with Japan's ever-expanding power.

Remarkably, Patton—the brilliant military analyst—seemed to predict Pearl Harbor years in advance in a memo titled "Surprise," which detailed his view of how easy the Japanese might (and presumably would) perform a surprise attack on the Hawaiian Islands. General George Patton's thinking was prescient and profound even between wars.

CHAPTER 3:
This Means War

"Duty is but discipline carried to its highest degree."

- General George S. Patton -

Although the Pattons were no longer stationed in Hawaii on December 7, 1941, when the Japanese launched a huge surprise attack on Pearl Harbor, it was a day that would "live in infamy," in the words of President Franklin Delano Roosevelt. Just a few months before this infamous date, George S. Patton was promoted to General, first as a Brigadier General on October 2nd, 1941, and then as a Major General on April 4th, 1941.

Even before the Japanese attack, the entire country seemed to be buzzing with war rumors as the entire nation eagerly monitored the events unfolding between the fascist Axis powers of Germany, Japan, and Italy. Beyond the general public's anxiety and speculation, war appeared to be a very serious option for the United States Military, one way or another.

Patton reportedly staged a major simulation drive of 1000 tanks from Columbus, Georgia to Panama City, Florida about a year before the attack on Pearl Harbor in December 1940. This was a rehearsal run for the extraordinary drive that General Patton would lead his tank battalions through just a few years later in France.

Yet, General Patton's first land invasion would take place in Africa, not Europe. General Dwight D. Eisenhower committed Patton to the conquest of North Africa under the codename "Operation Torch" in the summer of 1942. Patton led a force of 33,000 men who landed on the beaches of Casablanca in around 100 different landing craft.

They landed on November 8, 1942, and were met with rather severe resistance from the Nazi-orchestrated French forces of the "Vichy" puppet government that the Germans had erected shortly after France's Nazi conquest. Notwithstanding the opponents' fury, Patton made quick work of them, capturing Casablanca and negotiating a ceasefire on November 11th, 1942.

Patton was overjoyed; Casablanca would be seized entirely intact without another shot being fired, and to top it all off, it was the old General's birthday; the armistice was the nicest birthday gift he could have received. Casablanca, Morocco's harbor, was swiftly transformed into a military station, and the Casablanca Conference was held two months later.

The United Chiefs of Staff supervised the plans for the invasion of Sicily, striking directly at the Italian zone of control and initiating the liberation of Europe during this conference. Nevertheless, before Europe could be captured, the war for North Africa had to be won, and when Operation Torch had concluded, the next part of that mission began in the Tunisian campaign in February 1943, in a spot called the Kasserine Pass.

Trapped within the famed Atlas Mountains range, German General Erwin Rommel led his Afrika Korps against the Allied advance with a combined regiment of Italian Tanks and two Panzer divisions. In this operation, the Allied soldiers were severely ill-prepared and inexperienced, and were easily forced back by Rommel's forces.

Seeing that the deck needed to be reshuffled, military high command sought General George S. Patton to replace the inexperienced leadership. In March 1943, he took direct command of all American units in Tunisia. Despite the fact that Paton had already shown himself during the siege of Casablanca, his new charges' initial reactions to him were mixed.

During an introductory convocation to his new troops, he was seen as rude and obscene by these battle-tested veterans. Many of those who had only recently experienced the agony of combat starred in bewilderment as Patton promised them of the "beauty of death" on the battlefield. Patton's grim exhortation that these troops should fight until the "tank was blasted out from under them" and then fight "on foot" was like salt in their still-fresh wounds.

Instead of being inspired by these summons to arms, many of these battle-hardened men felt taken advantage of. According to one of the soldiers at the time, those who heard Patton's rant about the grandeur of pouring blood and having guts felt they would "give the blood" while Patton would "supply the guts." In fact, it was here that General Patton got the nickname that would stick with him for the remainder of the war: "Old Blood and Guts."

Notwithstanding some of the initial criticism directed at his deranged character, Paton was given clear instructions: turn around a lost and demoralized brigade in 10 days. For some, this may have appeared to be a massive effort, but for Patton, it was only a matter of routine. He approached the floundering unit from the bottom up.

He replaced their muddy and blood-stained attire with fresh, clean, and nicely pressed uniforms in order to give the entire group a total facelift, and with the apparent belief that a well-dressed soldier is a far more confident soldier. He then began drilling them around the clock in accordance with his own fast-paced program.

He returned these war veterans to square one by pressing the reset button. He brought them back to boot camp for those ten days so he could personally assess their strengths and weaknesses and then utilize all of his knowledge to shape them into a more effective fighting machine. This was Patton 101, and he expected them to breeze through his 10-day crash course.

His lesson plan's final exam was an uphill attack against the enemy position of Gafsa in Tunisia. General Patton was not disappointed, and on March 17th, 1943, they drove the Italian and German units out of El Guettar. Patton saw this as the gateway to the ultimate stepping stone to Europe: Sicily.

CHAPTER 4:
Operation Husky

"The object of war is not to die for your country but to make the other bastard die for his."

- General George S. Patton -

On July 10, 1943, General Patton and a force of 90,000 men converged on the Sicilian coastal resort of Licata. The unit was extremely effective, quickly capturing the beachfront while repelling coordinated German and Italian attacks. The fascists were eventually driven to the sea, and by the end of the conflict, with only 7,500 American casualties compared to the 113,000 enemy troops neutralized, it would appear that General Patton's command had yet another astounding success story.

Patton immediately cemented his control on the island after such a surprising victory, while the surviving German and Italian forces (about 100,000 in total) withdrew to Italy. With the enemy on the run, Patton's tired forces could recuperate and Patton could plan his next move. Even with his Axis opponents on the run, Patton's long-time adversary of controversy wasn't far behind.

Many events will soon erupt on the Sicilian island, turning it into a public relations nightmare. Patton created the first negative precedent when he cruelly shot and killed two mules and then beat their irate owner with a stick! The unfortunate Sicilian farmer had apparently briefly lost control of the farm animals, and they were on a bridge as Patton's armored column came. The farm animals seemed to freeze in place, like deer caught in headlights, fully obstructing Patton's unit's way.

Patton, never one for patience, pulled out his rifle and began shooting after screaming and cursing. That's then the owner, who was trying to herd the animals, appeared and began to regret Patton's actions bitterly. It's unclear whether Patton understood what the poor man was saying, but not appreciating the overall sound and tone of the man's sobs, Patton chose to whip him with a walking stick.

Patton then kicked his dead animals off the bridge and ordered his men to march forward when the man ran for shelter. One can only imagine whether this unlucky man had earlier celebrated his release from Italian tyrant Benito Mussolini, but after witnessing such savagery from the US forces, it's safe to say he had second thoughts.
But, it was not only the native Sicilians who bore the brunt of Patton's harshness; his own troops were frequently dealt blows from his iron fist, as witnessed by the infamous slapping episodes of Privates Charles H. Kuhl and Paul G. Bennet. These men clearly had war exhaustion, or what we now term Post Traumatic Stress Disorder (PTSD).

Patton wasn't buying it, no matter how shell-shocked these problematic soldiers appeared in their hospital beds. On two different visits, he slapped them both in the face and dismissed them as nothing more than whining cowards. Patton evidently refused to acknowledge the truth of allegations of war-induced mental problems such as PTSD, believing that he could somehow snap (or slap!) the stressed infantrymen out of it.

The adjacent doctors, however, did not take well to this rampaging General nonchalantly beating their patients, and once the violent occurrences reached the ears of General Dwight D. Eisenhower, Patton was ordered to stand down and even compelled to apologize. High command wanted Patton to make atonement for his wrongdoings, but they also wanted to cover for him, fearing that such flagrant abuses of authority would be exposed in the public.
Despite efforts to suppress the tale, it managed to get out and was making headlines in America by November 1943. Patton was forced to sit out for over a year as a result of all the negative attention.

Patton was treated fairly, considering that the regular strict process of the United States Military would have sought an immediate court-martial against Patton under normal circumstances.

In the end, it was only out of necessity that Eisenhower did not take harsher action against him. General Patton was his greatest eyes and ears on the battlefield, and the Allied forces could not afford to lose him, no matter how ridiculous his behavior was. Even so, it wouldn't be until January 26th that he'd be granted a second opportunity, with a new post in England preparing for the largest battle of his career: the Normandy invasion.

CHAPTER 5:
Invasion of Normandy

"I am a soldier, I fight where I am told, and I win where I fight."

- General George S. Patton -

Patton was surreptitiously spirited away to London while his latest battlefield scandal faded, and he was given command of a new army poised and ready to make history like never before. The United States "Third Army," a motorized brigade designed to be as flexible as possible, was set to crash into continental Europe in July 1944.

The Germans, the original architects of the blitzkrieg, feared Patton's own lightning-fast attack more than anybody else. By the summer of 1944, all German eyes were fixed on General Patton, so much so that US military intelligence devised a cunning ruse to throw the Germans off guard.

Despite the fact that the planned invasion had always been intended to take place on the western shores of France at Normandy, the United States began a concerted effort to send misinformation and false intelligence reports to German operatives that the planned invasion would instead take place in Pas de Calais in the north of France.

This Allied deception strategy even went so far as to form a "phantom army" with Hollywood-style props of phony boats and planes assembled on the British coast of Dover, parallel to Pas de Calais across the English Channel. Dover, in southeast England, would have been the most convenient launching place for an invasion of France, but the German high command should have known that this option was far too obvious for the Americans to consider.

However, under the guise of "Operation Fortitude," General Patton was told to keep a low profile while fake armaments were positioned all along the Dover coast so that German officials would believe that their dreaded adversary was planning an invasion from the Southeast Corner of England to Pas de Calais.

In the end, the ruse worked perfectly; the Axis was so convinced of an impending invasion of Pas de Calais that even after Patton and his men landed in Normandy, some 150 miles away, the Nazis refused to reinforce the position and kept their battalions fully in place, facing off against the phantom army that never arrived.

Patton's force landed for the first time in July and was on the mainland by August 1st, 1944. Patton was resolved to use his speed and aggression to his maximum advantage in this assault. Patton's major strategy was to send scout units ahead of the main army to explore the enemy's weaknesses; he would then dispatch "self-propelled artillery" to move in on these places as the armored column advanced.

The main issue was that the entire German army was so brilliantly camouflaged in French terrain that entire German regiments would frequently blend in and vanish right in the middle of a French farm or hedgerow. With the Germans concealing their main army until midnight, a persistent game of cat and mouse ensued between German convoys and the Allied Air Force that intended to destroy them.

Even more lethal were the sniper sites and pill boxes strewn over the landscape, where trained German marksmen could remain safe from the fray, high up in trees with expertly hidden ladders ready for a speedy escape, as death rained down from above. Notwithstanding these challenges, Patton's forces marched ahead in rapid succession.
This quick progress would last until August 31st, 1944, when his Third Army's tanks encountered a gasoline deficit on the outskirts of Metz. According to those who observed it, Patton's tanks, trucks, and

jeeps all came to a standstill one by one when each vehicle ran out of gas. The infantry were immediately ordered out of the trucks they were riding in and to walk.

After assessing the severe fuel shortage, Patton began bombarding Eisenhower with telegrams, demanding to know why he wasn't given enough gasoline to fulfill his job. He allegedly informed Eisenhower that "his forces would gladly forego food and even weapons if they could simply get oil."

Many hungry soldiers would probably disagree with the statement made on their behalf, but Patton's offer of food in exchange for oil would fall on deaf ears regardless; High Command had other plans for their scarcely-allocated resources, and granting Patton another valiant charge was not one of them. Patton had little alternative but to park his tanks and have his men dig in their heels, strengthening the territory they already possessed as they busied themselves erecting fortifications on large swaths of country from Luxembourg to Nancy.
Patton's march was halted for the time being. Some speculated that Eisenhower purposely curtailed Patton's fuel supply in order to maintain some control over the crazy commander. Concerned that if Old Blood and Guts had enough gasoline, he wouldn't stop until he reached Berlin and beyond—a feat that the Allied Command wasn't yet prepared for—it was decided to end the arrogant General's career early.

This brief pause in action, however, allowed the local German soldiers to re-evaluate and bolster their positions. As a result, when Patton's Third Army finally confronted the fortified defenses in Metz in November, it was virtually a stalemate with significant deaths on both sides.

Patton temporarily halted his forces before sending them to overrun Fort Driant to the south of Metz, but the assault force was badly defeated by the fanatically resisting Germans. Patton's forces couldn't break through the impregnable concrete with their long guns blazing.

Patton trimmed his losses and abandoned the Fort Driant effort after losing six tanks, 50 soldiers, and nearly 300 more wounded, dismissing his defeat as a simple "technical experiment that did not succeed."

In any case, the seizure of Fort Driant was a rather insignificant action with no critical strategic significance. Patton recognized this fact when he surrendered to the Germans, who were already trapped and entombed like the dead inside their gigantic concrete fort. He continued on, he and his men steadily marching west.

CHAPTER 6:
The Battle of the Bulge

"Lead me, follow me, or get out of my way."

- *General George S. Patton* -

The Battle of the Bulge was Germany's final attempt to change the direction of the war. With significant losses in the east fighting the Russians and the fast approaching Allies in the west, Germany was under attack from two ways at the same time. The Battle of the Bulge was a last-ditch effort to break free from the vice that was squeezing Germany.

On December 16, 1944, German tanks and artillery that had previously been buried deep within the Ardennes Forest were unleashed in a frenzied drive to face the American army front on. Eisenhower summoned an emergency meeting with Patton and many other Generals and officers to examine the situation.

When Eisenhower asked Patton how long it would take him to mount an effective counterattack against the German assault, all eyes were on him. Patton didn't waste any time in responding, declaring, "as soon as you're done with me." Eisenhower dismissed this remark as more empty bragging from Patton and insisted on waiting until a few days later, on December 22nd, when his forces would be better equipped to meet the approaching German onslaught.

When Patton exited the meeting, he immediately summoned his command staff and famously told them to "play ball." These were the predetermined code words that Patton had directed his staff to use before meeting with Eisenhower, signaling them to quickly begin mobilizing and preparing for the German counter-offensive.

Patton's troops met up with the resurgent Germans on December 26th, the day after Christmas. Patton's forces were initially dug in deep in their positions, doing everything they could to avoid enemy fire, but it wasn't long before the Germans were used as target practice as their infantry launched a daring assault out of the woodland at the Allied line.

The weather was against them, and because they were knee-deep in snow, their charge quickly devolved into a trudge through the elements that slowed them down. Patton's forces found it quite easy to pick off these Germans who were literally swimming in the snow. They attempted again and again, but each time they were greeted with lethal results at the hands of Patton's army.

They were soon in full retreat, and Patton arrived in the bombed-out town of Bastogne to provide a corridor to rescue the embattled American battalions besieged there. The courageous rescue of these previously enslaved individuals ended the Battle of the Bulge, and the Germans were once again driven back across the Rhine.

Patton ultimately gave chase on March 22nd, having his engineers construct a pontoon bridge across the Rhine. Patton was taking his time at this point, and allegedly urinated right into the river as he walked across. The men of Patton's Third Army appeared to be in clear sailing at first, but as the hours passed, his forces advancing across the Rhine were ultimately recognized by what was left of the German Air Force.

Shortly after, several of the Luftwaffe's last remaining Messerschmitt fighters began harassing Patton's advancing columns of infantry. The Nazi pilots would fly daringly low and then dive at oncoming infantry while firing machine guns.

However, the tactic cost the German pilots far more than any casualties caused on Patton's brigade; astonishingly, the Third Army's exceptionally powerful anti-aircraft weaponry shot down all 33 assaulting Messerschmitt jets that day.

Patton began to plan their next move after their way had been cleared. Patton turned his sights on a nearby POW camp and devised

a plan to rescue the inmates, believing that momentum was on their side and that they now had the time and means to accomplish so. Patton convened what would become known as "Task Force Baum" on March 26th, 1945, named after the 23-year-old Captain Abraham J. Baum whom Patton had commissioned to oversee the expedition.
This would-be liberator task group consisted of 16 tanks and 314 troops. Many cautioned Patton that 314 soldiers would not be enough to take such a heavily walled stronghold, but Patton, ever prepared to put his luck (and others' patience) to the test, launched the daring mission nevertheless. Task Force Baum was dispatched 50 miles behind enemy lines to liberate captives from a fortified prisoner of war camp on Hammelburg's outskirts.

The German opposition dug into this compound was severe, as many of his enemies had predicted; over half of Task Force Baum were killed on their first approach. Moreover, once the task force's remaining soldiers managed to crash through the main gate, they mistaken numerous Serbian inmates still wearing their military uniforms for guards and slaughtered several of them accidently due to a mix of weariness and personal ignorance.

General Gunther Von Guckel, one of the genuine Germans in charge of defending the compound, who felt sorry for the Serbs who were being killed by the Americans, ordered some of his American Prisoners to approach the task force's befuddled participants and explain the situation.

As the American POWs were able to fill in the blanks, General Gunther and the majority of the other German guards used the opportunity to depart the compound entirely. The task force chose not to pursue them and instead concentrated on releasing the detainees. It was then that they discovered General Patton's ultimate goal in launching this mission: Colonel Waters, Patton's son-in-law.
Running through the front gate with a white surrender flag in his hand, flanked by one of the few remaining German officers, it was supposed to be Task Force Baum's moment of triumph, when they

could report back to Patton that they had succeeded in rescuing the Colonel, let alone the hundreds of other detainees they had freed.

Nevertheless, as fate would have it, things would take a turn for the worst when gunshots burst out of nowhere from one remaining German guard who had been hidden and waiting in the background. The Colonel merely got a flesh wound and would recover, but the damage made him unable to walk, adding to the mission's risks.

The most obvious issue was the huge number of inmates they had freed, as they had underestimated the number of POWs imprisoned at the camp. The task force rapidly recognized that their cars could not possibly transport all of them. They had to load nearly 700 people inside and on top of multiple tanks and trucks in their first try. The German army caught them in this state of severe disorganization and led a devastating counterattack. The Germans mercilessly retrieved their POWs, picking them right out of the cars, and even added more to their collection from Task Force Baum's failed rescuers.

In the end, only 35 of the heroic souls who conducted this rescue returned safely. The mission was a total flop. In later evidence, Patton said that his failure to free this single POW camp was the only mistake he made throughout the war. Old Blood and Guts' war record was otherwise flawless by the time Germany surrendered on May 9th, 1945.

CHAPTER 7:
An Old Man's War

"Anyone in any walk of life who is content with mediocrity is untrue to himself and to American tradition."

- George S. Patton -

Most Americans felt optimistic about the future in the spring of 1945. Their war effort, both at home and on the battlefields abroad, appeared to be fruitful and yielding tremendous returns. America had faced up to the world's most cruel authoritarian force and was not only successful, but appeared to be on the verge of a great win.

The death of the political person who led them there was the last thing they expected to hear in what should have been a national moment of victory. When word of President Franklin Delano Roosevelt's death circulated on April 12th, 1945, it came as a huge shock to everyone. For many years, FDR, as he was affectionately known, had been a part of the American consciousness.

In reality, F.D.R. was the only US President to be elected four times, which led to the usual two-term limit for succeeding US presidents. F.D.R. and his fireside talks were clearly engraved on the minds of all Americans at the time. He was not only the United States' commander-in-chief during World War II, but he also guided the country through the Great Depression and every other national crisis of the last two decades.

General George S. Patton, for one, was as surprised as everyone else to get the news. As prescient as his statements have been in the past regarding other crises, he had not seen this one coming. That same day, he had been touring the horrors of newly liberated concentration camps, where the blood of recently executed prisoners trickled over the floorboards, neatly arranged like pieces of wood in the corner.

The horror of all of this was compounded later that day when Patton learned of the death of his President, a man he sincerely admired. According to all accounts, this admiration was mutual, with F.D.R. frequently referring to Patton as "Old Cavalryman" and even noting on occasion that Patton was "Our Greatest Battle General."

Patton was filled with grief at the departure of a man he highly respected, while also filled with dread at the prospect of his successor, a man he despised, Harry S. Truman, taking over the final days of the war effort. Paton was summoned to a meeting with his immediate superiors, Generals Omar Bradley and Dwight Eisenhower, shortly after learning of the President's death.

They had chosen an abandoned salt mine unearthed just days before by Patton's forces as the location for their meeting. The Nazis utilized the mine as a last-minute hideout to store millions of dollars in money, gold bars, and famous items of art. Before deciding what to do with the buried wealth, Eisenhower wanted to assess it with his generals.

Patton was as macabre as usual as he pointed out the perilous nature of the thin rope the three men's elevator fell on as the rickety wooden elevator took them down to the deep black depths below. "If that clothesline breaks," he remarked cynically, "promotions in the United States Army should be significantly boosted!"

Eisenhower, on the other hand, was not in the mood for his weird comedy and promptly shut him off with, "George, that's enough! There will be no more wisecracks till we are above ground!" All kidding aside, Patton realized that the thin silver cord from which their elevator was suspended served all too well to reflect the dangerous position in which they were all in.

Despite the fact that they had won the war, their President had died, and now three of the most important men in the United States military, one of whom was a future president himself, were kilometers deep beneath German soil, trapped in an ever-increasing shroud of darkness. All of these bleak details seemed to perfectly set the tone for the world that would emerge after WWII.

CHAPTER 8:
Watch Your Mouth

"Moral courage is the most valuable and usually the most absent characteristic in men."

- General George S. Patton -

As World War II came to an end and the lines of Europe began to appear, Patton could clearly see the shattered lines of the Allies emerge as well. Even as the Germans surrendered, Patton realized that the next threat would come from Russia and its doctrine of communist world dominance.

Dwight D. Eisenhower, on the other hand, had his own concerns, and more than Russia, he feared an enraged General Patton causing a diplomatic disaster on the world stage. To distract the outspoken General from his idle political intrigue, Eisenhower appointed Patton as Military Governor of Bavaria, far from the other international participants in the postwar peace.

It was believed that by transporting him secretly to a Bavarian estate with its own swimming pool, bowling hall, and even two yachts, the conqueror of Western Europe would be distracted enough to keep his mouth shut. When he gazed over the German hills, Patton wished for one more battle with his army at full strength.

Patton considered pursuing a transfer to the Pacific to at least see out the last combat in the still-raging struggle against the Japanese. More than that, Patton continued to advocate for the United States to militarily engage its ostensible eastern ally, the Russians, which was unimaginable at the time.

This was before the Cold War and the Iron Curtain fell on Europe. Official US policy at the time was that "Russia was our friend," and anyone who had doubts about the relationship should keep them to themselves. Patton, much to Eisenhower's and the rest of the high command's chagrin, refused to toe this line.

He is believed to have told journalists about his connections with the Russians, "you cannot lay down with a diseased jackal." He did not hold back or use any political subtlety. We will never do business with the Russians. "Let us keep our boots shined and bayonets honed, and project a picture of force and strength to these people." If you fail to do so, I regret to inform you that we won the battle against the Germans but lost the war." When Eisenhower learned of Patton's latest gaffe, he was enraged, believing that such remarks were provocative and potentially dangerous incitements to a nation that he still thought would be a potential ally and partner in the peace process.

Eisenhower intended to hide such harsh rhetoric from his Generals, but according to some stories, the Kremlin was fully aware of Patton's critiques of their regime, which had landed this American General on the NKVD's watch list. A Soviet General personally visited Patton at his Bavarian headquarters not long after this Russian spying began.

The Soviet Field Marshal General entered Patton's office absolutely unannounced, escorted by his shocked Chief of Staff. Following a brief introduction, the Russian General offered Patton a series of demands and criticisms of his men's behavior. The fact that so many Germans had been allowed to flee the Russians and seek safety in the American area of the occupation was of special concern.

This was extremely common since the Germans believed that the Americans would treat them considerably more humanely than the vengeful Russians, who were already well renowned for their cruelty against German people. The Russian General specifically mentioned German boatmen who were ferrying hundreds of German refugees across the Danube and into the safety of the American Zone.

The Russian General then asserted that these boats and their operators were Russian property because they were leaving the Russian Zone, and requested that Patton immediately return these soldiers and their boats to the Russians. The Chief of Staff for Patton recalls the deafening quiet in the room after the ultimatum was issued.

Patton glared coldly at the Russian General as he carefully removed the Cuban cigar he had been smoking from his mouth and placed it in his ashtray. Still staring emotionlessly at the Russian in front of him, he silently opened his desk drawer and brought out his custom-made Smith and Wesson.357 handgun.

Patton slapped the handgun down on his desk, his previously peaceful visage bursting in rage as he roared, "get this son of a bitch out of here!" Who on earth let him in? "Do not allow any more Russian thugs into this headquarters!" He immediately went to his Chief of Staff and yelled, "Alert the Fourth, Eleventh, and Sixty-Fifth Divisions for an attack to the east!"

Even the most hardened Soviet general looked horrified at this time, convinced that General Patton had officially authorized World War Three. The previously imposing Field Marshal from the East, according to all accounts, was scared to death as Patton's Chief of Staff immediately led him out of the room.

But, despite their wild antics, they had all failed to call the General's bluff. When the Chief of Staff returned, believing that they were on the approach of a full-fledged war with Russia, he was perplexed to find the previously angry Patton entirely comfortable and smiling. "How was that?" he inquired.

"Sometimes you have to put on a show, and I'm not going to let any Soviet marshal, general, or private tell me what I have to do," Patton added, as his Chief of Staff started in startled silence. "Call off the alert," Patton said, "that'll be the last we hear from those bastards."

This was, in fact, the final time Patton would be questioned by the Russians; he would be dead in a matter of months.

CHAPTER 9:
Man of Controversy

"Say what you mean, and mean what you say."

- General George S. Patton -

General George S. Patton was a man who spoke his thoughts and frequently sparked controversy in the process. Many saw his ability as a "straight shooter" as both his greatest advantage and his worst liability. The worst of Patton's rants, without a doubt, occurred when he disparaged the same individuals he worked so hard to save - Nazi Holocaust survivors.

Patton was in charge of the displaced people who survived the camps as Governor of Bavaria. Patton would frequently express his anger with the Jews, Gypsies, Russians, Hungarians, and Poles he was in charge of. He once made the absurd judgment that the displaced persons under his supervision were clad in filthy rags and smelled awful.

Of course, anyone with a little common sense would recognize that after months or perhaps years in a concentration camp, deprived of even the most basic essentials, hygiene would not be the first priority. The fact that the displaced people entrusted in his care were still wearing dirty prisoner clothes provided by the Nazis was a fact that could only be blamed on General Patton.

As he was indignantly talking about how unattractive the captives appeared, he was the one who was denying them fresh clothing. Nevertheless, Patton's aggressive attitude toward the very people he rescued was only the tip of the iceberg. Patton will soon express his deep disgust and contempt for the military.
On one particular occasion, Eisenhower escorted Patton to a synagogue on Yom Kippur, most likely to bridge the cultural barrier

between Patton and his detainees. For the most part, the General restrained himself, although Patton later remarked, "we entered the synagogue, which was crammed with the largest disgusting mass of humanity I have ever seen." Of course, I've seen them since the beginning and marveled at the fact that people said to be created in the image of God may look or act the way they do."

Patton's remarks are revolting in the extreme, and it is difficult for most people to believe that the same man regarded by many as Europe's valiant liberator could utter such heinous things. Patton's harshness did not stop with his comments; he was later heavily chastised for placing former Nazis in the same DP camps as Holocaust survivors.

Worse, there is evidence that Patton gave former Nazis—the very people from whom he had rescued the other displaced persons—preferential treatment and, in some cases, specific supervisory duties over others in the camp. Things had become so awful that Holocaust survivors could be forgiven for thinking they had simply been transferred from a German-styled concentration camp to a General George Patton-styled one.

As word circulated about the horrific treatment of refugees at Patton's DP camps, outside campaigners began to speak up. In order to gain the support of freshly elected President Harry Truman, a special mission led by former immigration official Earl Harrison was dispatched to tour Patton's camps. They were shocked to see that the allegations concerning the treatment of migrants were well-founded.

Patton's actions were immediately called into question after a damning report was returned to D.C., and steps were taken to better the life of the detained refugees. Patton's only reason for treating the displaced people in his camp more like captives under armed guard than liberated citizens was that it was for their own security.

According to Patton, if the displaced persons (DPs) were not kept under custody, they would "spread throughout the land like locusts, and would eventually have to be picked up after quite a few of them had been slain and quite a few Germans murdered and pillaged."

As grim and unpleasant as Patton's images could be, this was his justification. He claimed to be saving both the DPs and the average German citizen, believing that if Holocaust survivors were allowed to roam freely, chaos would erupt and they would be targeted by angry Germans, and in turn, the DPs would seek revenge on ordinary German citizens, robbing and killing them at will.

This was Patton's justification for putting thousands of people under barbed wire and armed guards around the clock. Eisenhower, on the other hand, was not convinced, and on September 28th, 1945, he officially dismissed Patton from his Military Governorship of Bavaria. On October 7th, almost a week later, Hitler entirely removed Patton from his position of command of the entire Third Army.

Patton was subsequently assigned to the Fifteenth United States Army, a small office staff tasked with producing a history of the war in Europe. Patton was first pleased with the task because of his professed interest in history, but without any direct action, he became bored and restless.

During the last few months of his life, he began to wander aimlessly about Western Europe, visiting Paris on occasion, Luxembourg and Brussels, and even visiting Stockholm, Sweden on one occasion, when he ran into some of the competitors he competed with in the 1912 Olympics. It was also during this time that he started hunting. The enjoyment of this innocent activity would shortly lead to General George S. Patton's death.

CHAPTER 10:
The Last Days of Patton

"How awful war is. Think of the waste."

- *General George S. Patton* -

The comments above were spoken by Patton just moments before a 2-ton military truck drove into the car in which he was riding, throwing the General into the air and banging his skull against the thick glass partition that divided the back of his specially prepared Cadillac from the front. The powerful crash fractured his nose and severed his spinal cord in a matter of seconds.

As the destroyed car came to a stop and gravity pulled Patton back to his feet, his now entirely numb body sagged and slumped to the side of the road on its own. Patton was aware that he was paralyzed, unable to feel anything below the neck. General Hobart Gay, his friend, was in the backseat with him. Patton and Gay went out on a simple pheasant hunt in the German countryside.

General Patton felt more like he was hunted after becoming paralyzed and absolutely helpless. An ambulance arrived on the scene shortly after the incident and transported Patton to the recently created U.S. Army 130th Station Hospital. Patton's health appeared to be rapidly deteriorating upon arrival; blood had drained from his face, and he was no longer responsive.

Patton would spend the next two weeks in a hospital bed, his upper body wrapped in a plaster cast to relieve the terrible pressure on his spine while the hospital searched the globe for a neurosurgeon. Dr. Glen Spurling, a U.S.-based expert in the discipline, was eventually chosen by the hospital staff.
An all-points bulletin was sent to locate this neurosurgeon, and it was quickly established that he was aboard a train traveling from

Kentucky to Washington, D.C. Dr. Spurling was then apprehended in Cincinnati and quickly flew out to examine Patton after being briefed on his condition.

Yet, all of these attempts would be futile in the end. General George S. Patton died gently on December 21, 1945, of a pulmonary embolism caused by his weakened immobility. In a sublime irony, the General, who had always been restless and full of activity, died as a result of staying too still.

According to his wife Beatrice, who sat at his side after being brought in from the United States, he died shortly after she told him a goodnight tale. Patton had a lifelong desire to be read to since he was a child, which some attribute to his juvenile dyslexia, which caused him to crave people to read the spoken word that he occasionally struggled with.

In any case, this was the last thing Beatrice would do with her husband; after a few moments, he simply stated, "I'm becoming asleep." "Why don't you go eat your dinner, and we'll complete the chapter when you return?" Beatrice then obeyed her husband and went down to the cafeteria for her dinner, leaving Patton to sleep.
He'd fallen asleep and wouldn't wake up. Beatrice Patton was grieved, of course, but the Patton family, long known for their love for the mystical, are claimed to have had a strange premonition even before their patriarch's injuries that he wouldn't be returning to them after the war.

Patton himself alluded to these ominous signs, claiming that his "luck had run out" and that he would die on the battlefield. Patton was a firm believer in reincarnation, constantly referring to previous lifetimes he had experienced.

His daughter, Ruth Ellen, would later tell of waking on the morning of Patton's death in the United States, only to see the old General standing exactly at the foot of her bed. She reported that as her gaze met his, he merely grinned and vanished.

It's up to us whether we believe these anecdotal stories or not, but one thing is certain: this larger-than-life and complicated American figure has a legacy that will live on - in whatever shape or form it takes.

CONCLUSION

Much has been said in recent years regarding the possibility that General Patton was slain because of his outspoken, and often downright insulting, ideas. According to these conspiracy theorists, the military truck colliding with Patton's Cadillac was no accident, but rather a planned hit carried out by, well, just about anyone.

Early on, there were allegations that the Russian secret service planned to assassinate Patton for his critical remarks about the Soviet Union, as well as for the manner he treated some Russian generals. There is also speculation that Patton was intentionally bumped off by America's own military, which had been unhappy with Patton's behavior for some years.

Others speculate about potential Nazi saboteurs; the list goes on and on. However, Patton's family and friends (including those who were with him on the day of the accident) have always maintained that Patton's death was the consequence of a car accident and nothing more.

These definitive claims from those closest to him, however, have not been enough to silence conspiracy theorists and the now-endless books and movies, such as Bill O'Reilly's "Killing Patton," which have endlessly speculated on what the "real" reason of Patton's demise might have been.

According to many who knew him best, the true cause was a car accident that resulted in a pulmonary embolism. For some who perceive something much more dynamic, something akin to a great Greek play, Patton was stabbed in the back by any number of plausible Brutus'.

Printed in Great Britain
by Amazon

50183459R00024